Pete the Cat

and the Cool Cat Boogie

For Amelia Swan—the girl
who loves to dance!
Eccl 3:4
—J.D. & K.D.

ISBN 978-1-338-60489-4

12 11 10 9 8 7 6 5 4 3 2 1   19 20 21 22 23 24

Printed in the U.S.A.   40

First Scholastic printing, September 2019

The artist used pen and ink with watercolor and acrylic paint on 300lb hot press paper to create
the illustrations for this book.
Typography by Jeanne L. Hogle

Pete the Cat was learning a new dance—
the COOL Cat Boogie!
Then Grumpy Toad came along.
"I really dig that song but Pete, you dance
all wrong!"
Pete did not know what to say. He just
turned and walked away.

Pete couldn't sleep at all that night!
"What if Grumpy Toad was right?
What if my moves are bad?"
The thought of NOT dancing made
Pete feel sad.

"Dancing is like magic!
When I hear a groovy beat
I'm full of happy in my feet!

I won't give up!

I love to dance.

Let me give it one more chance."

Pete was practicing the Cool Cat Boogie when he saw Squirrel.
"Hey, Squirrel,

How do you dance?
How do you groove?

Can you teach me how to move?"

"Sure, Pete! It's a simple song.

Just cha-cha-cha and dance along!"

Pete did not know
what to say.
He just turned
and walked away.

"But dancing is like magic! When I hear
a groovy beat I'm full of HAPPY in my feet!

I won't give up!
I love to dance.

Let me give it one more chance."

Pete was still practicing the Cool
Cat Boogie when Gus came along.

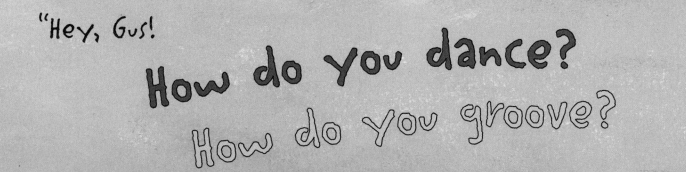

"Sure, Pete!
It's a simple song.

Just do the robot and
dance along!"

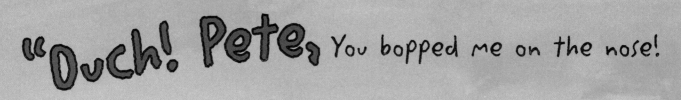

"Ouch! Pete, you bopped me on the nose! That is not how this dance goes!"

Pete did not know
what to say. He just
turned and walked away.

"But dancing is like magic!

When I hear a groovy beat I'm full of HAPPY in my feet!

I won't give up!
I love to dance.
Let me give it one more chance."

Pete was still trying to do the Cool Cat Boogie when Turtle came along.

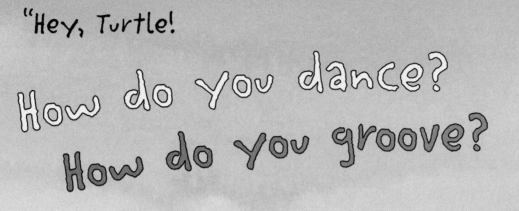

"Hey, Turtle!
How do you dance?
How do you groove?
Can you teach me how to move?"

"Sure, Pete!
It's a simple song.

Just shake your tail
and dance along!"

Pete felt like giving up.

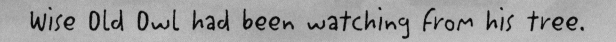
Wise Old Owl had been watching from his tree.

"Pete, it doesn't matter how you move as long as you are being you!"

"You are right!!!
I never want to
miss a chance
to dance!"

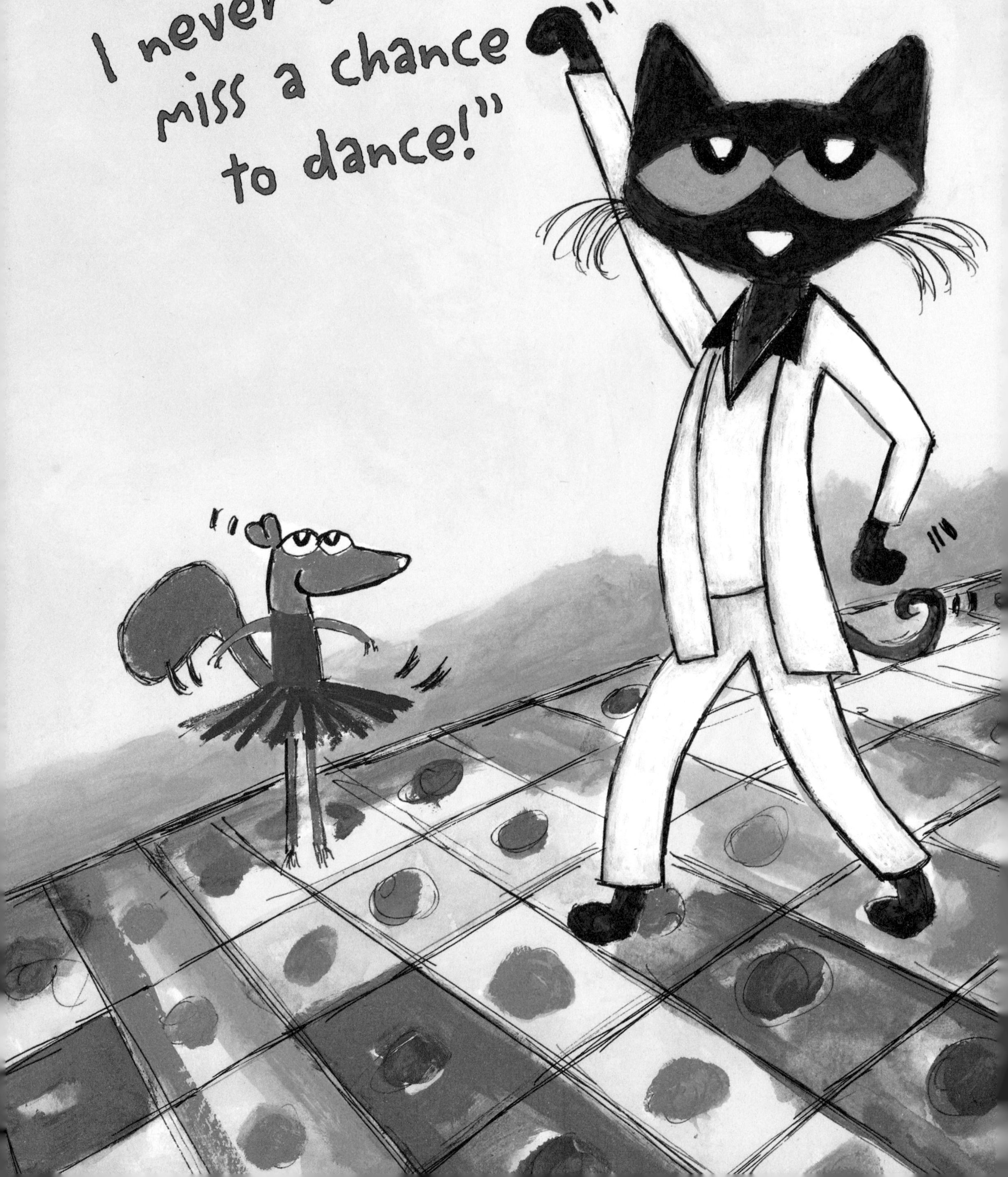

"When you hear a groovy beat and you feel happy in your feet, just dance,

DANCE, DANCE, DANCE."

Cool Cat Boogie

> I want to boogie with you.
> Grab your boogie shoes!

1.

2.

slide right...shake your tail → ← slide left...shake your tail

5.

6.

7.

rock and roll   jump back   rock and roll

3.

now clap, clap, clap
real smooth, you've got the groove

4.

jump front

8.

that's neat
you got the beat

9.

grab your air guitar
and rock it out like Pete

Katie McGee

In 2004, **Kimberly & James Dean** sat down at their kitchen table to work on a children's book together. Their dream finally became a reality with the release of *Pete the Cat and His Magic Sunglasses*. Both left corporate jobs in the late nineties (James was an electrical engineer, Kimberly worked in the press office of the governor of Georgia) to pursue their passion for art, and they have experienced a life made up of strange and wonderful coincidences ever since. Pete the Cat has brought magic into their lives. They work in side-by-side studios in Savannah, sharing their home with five cats and Emma the pug.